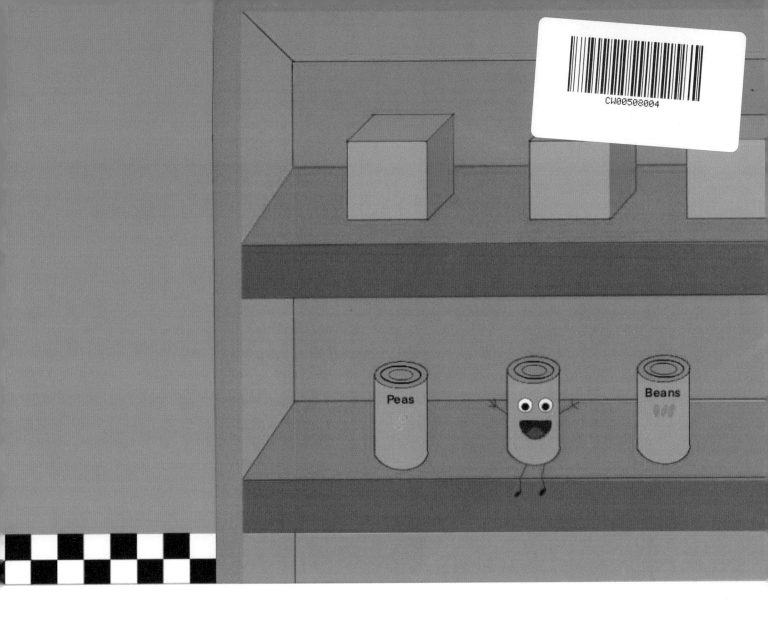

Tim can, the tin can, sat on his shop shelf everyday waiting for someone to take him home.

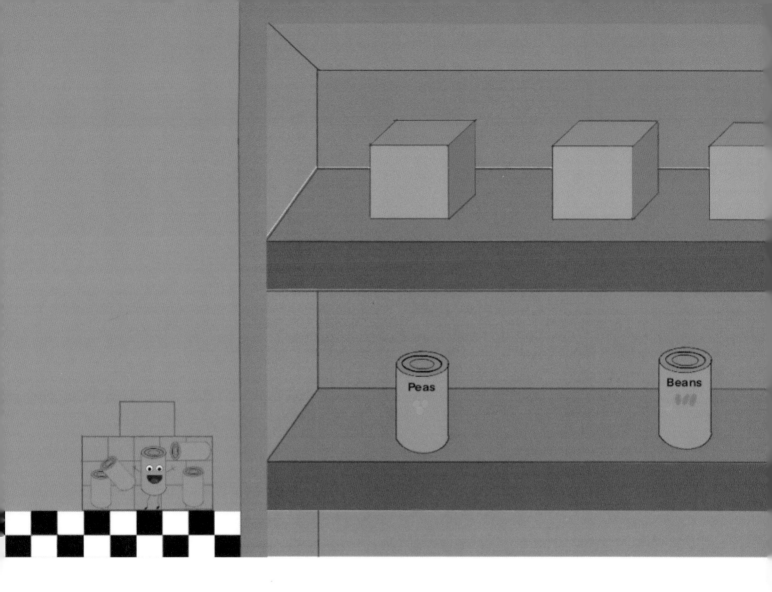

One day Tim Can was finally chosen to go home. He was thrown into the basket and was bought at the till.

Later that day Tim Can was emptied so his beans could be used for dinner. Tim was so excited.

Until he was thrown
in the wrong bin.

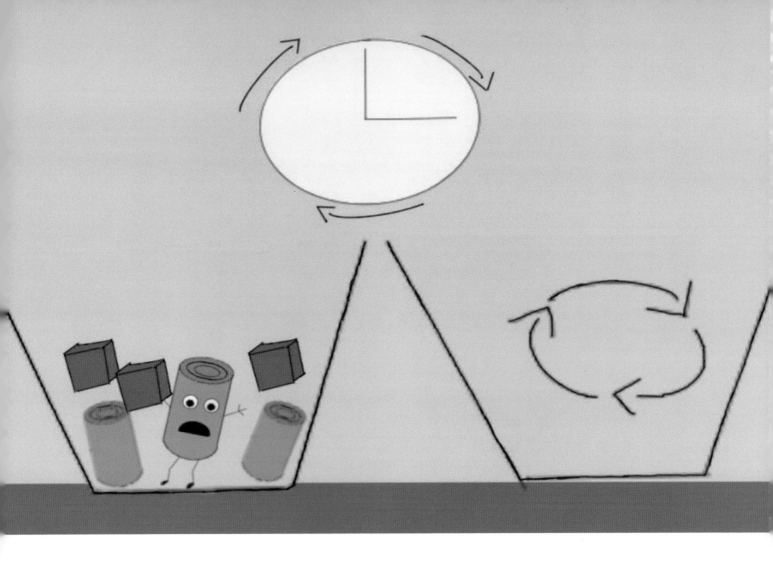

He waited and waited for someone to put him in the right bin. But nobody did.

**Bin Van**

The next day was bin day
and Tim was thrown into
the bin van.

Bin Van

But he quickly climbed out before he was taken to the wrong place.

Tim decided that he would walk to the recycling centre.

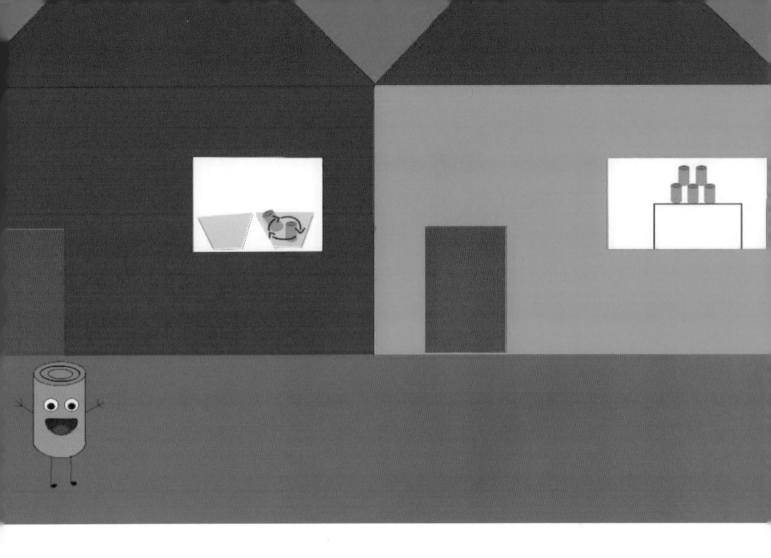

He walked past houses and could see other tin cans being reused or placed in the right bin. This made him happy.

He saw a tin can being used
as a pencil holder.

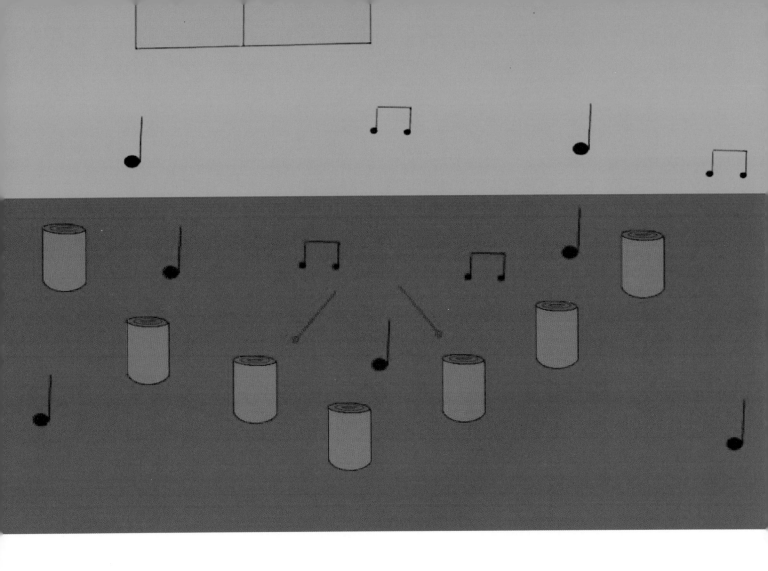

He saw tin cans being used
as a drum kit.

He saw all sorts of ways that tin cans have been reused and recycled.

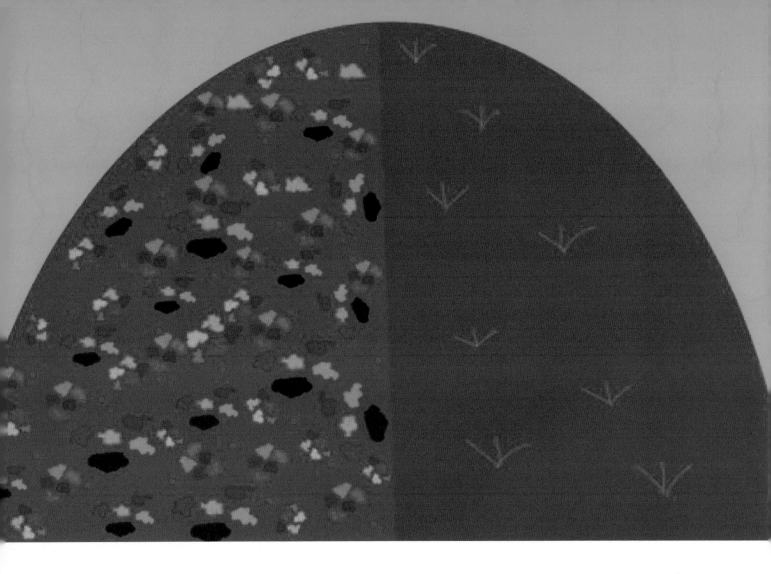

Then he came across the dumping ground. With lots of rubbish in the mud.

He would have ended up here.
This place was smelly. So Tim
Can ran away.

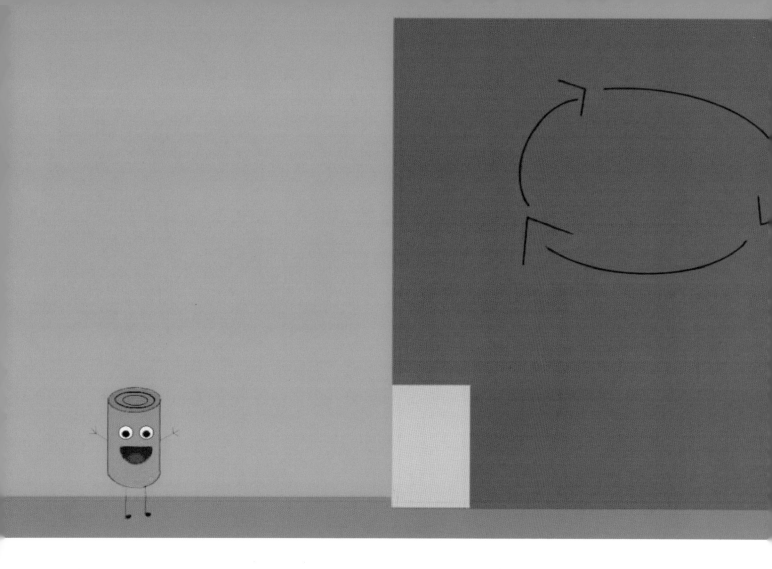

Tim Can finally arrived at the recycling centre.

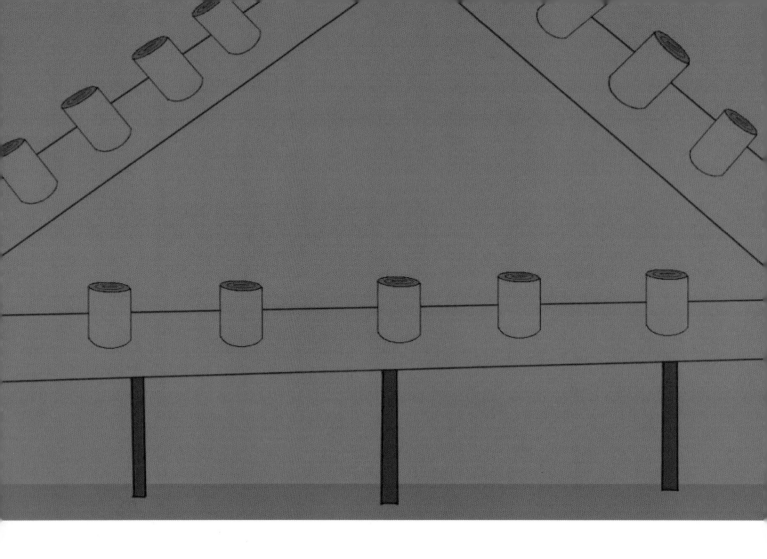

Tim walked in and saw tin cans everywhere.
Zooming along the shelves.

The tin cans moved towards a machine.
They went in one end as cans.

Then the tin cans came out the other end. But they looked different.

Tim Can went into the magic changing machine.

He came out the other side. He looked different. He was shorter and wider.

He wondered what he
would be used for next.

He was taken to a new place
and filled with sweetcorn.

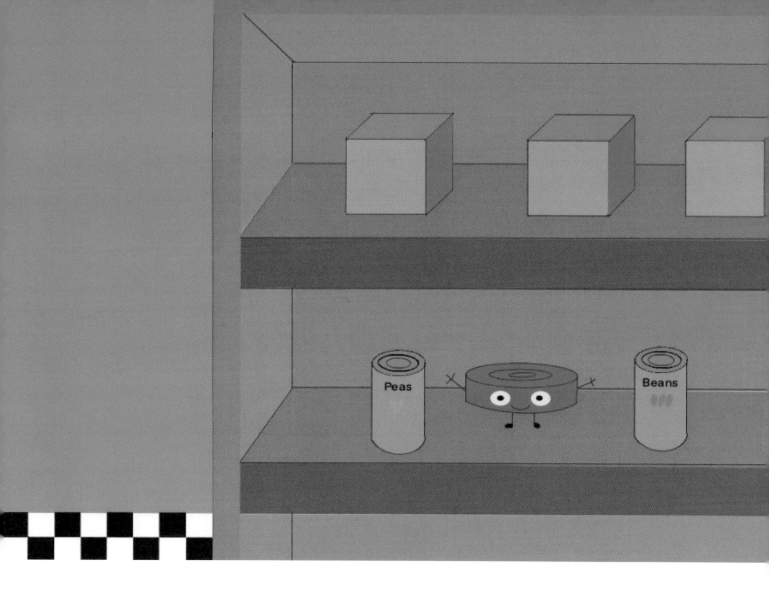

Now Tim Can is back on the shelf waiting to start his journey again.

# The
# End

Printed in Great Britain
by Amazon

31386598R00016